pulverize ('pəl-və-rīz) (v) What you can do to a snowball when you hit it with a baseball bat. Very cool, by the way.

retaliation (ri-ta-lē-'ā-shən)(n) Did I mention the **revenge** I'm going to get on my brother? Another word for that is retaliation, because anything so awesome should have more than one name!

revenge (rē-'venj) (n) Another name for the tricks I'm going to play on my annoying older brother. Sweet revenge will be **mine!**

slumber ('sləm-bər)(v) What you do when you're asleep. Before I slumber, though, I need to get some revenge on my brother.

subterfuge ('səb-tər-fyüj) (n) A clever trick you can use to get what you want. And what I want is revenge on my brother (see revenge). Did I say that alreddy?

CALVIN
GETS THE LAST
WORD

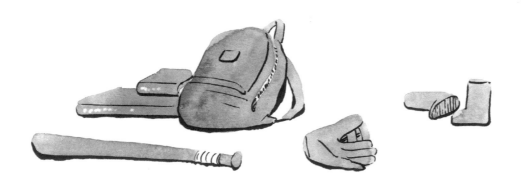

CALVIN GETS THE LAST WORD

Story by Margo Sorenson   Illustrations by Mike Deas

See that kid reading a book? That's Calvin. And I'm the book.
I'm Calvin's dictionary, and I'm tired.

If you were Calvin's dictionary, you'd be tired, too.

Why? Because Calvin loves words—I mean REALLY loves words.

That means he has to find *exactly* the right word for
everything—especially his rascally brother.

Just wait till you see what happens.

In the morning, Calvin brings me to the breakfast table.

His tricky brother waits to tell a joke until
the very second that Calvin gulps his milk.

So, Calvin snorks his milk out his nose!

PBTTTTHT!

That's why my page that reads **revenge** has milk spilled on it.

But Calvin knows that's not exactly the right word for his brother, although it sounds interesting.

On the school bus, everyone is pushing and yelling and shouting, running up and down the aisle, throwing backpacks.

That's when my page that reads **mayhem** gets torn.

But Calvin knows that word doesn't *quite*
fit his brother, though it's close.

At school, Calvin shoves me under his desk. The teacher asks Calvin a hard question about the Nile River, and Calvin sinks down in his chair.

That's why my page that reads **bewilderment** is wrinkled.

But Calvin knows that word has nothing to do with his brother.

Calvin carries me under his arm to the school library. When the librarian isn't looking, he and his friends write notes to each other, like "Pass me some bubble gum."

Of course, my page reading **subterfuge** is stuck to another page now.

Somehow, Calvin knows that doesn't work for his brother, either.

But it does help him think . . . .

On the way home, Calvin puts me on the seat next to him.

When one of the big kids grabs a little kid's pencil box,
Calvin grabs it away from him and gives it back to her.

Now you know why the page that reads **courageous** has pencil scribbles on it.

Calvin thinks there is no way that's the right word for his brother—
but maybe for himself . . . .

Calvin even hauls me along in his bat bag to baseball practice. He loves to crush the ball during batting practice, sending it over the fence.

That's why the page that reads **pulverize** has grass stains on it.

Calvin knows that although that word *could* work, not to mention it would be fun, it's not going to be exactly the perfect word for his brother.

dad
a
b c def
retaliation
calvin

At the dinner table, Calvin puts me next to his plate.
His brother waits to tell another joke until the very
moment Calvin's mouth is full.

Wouldn't you know it—Calvin sprays broccoli everywhere!

That's why my page with **retaliation** has green bumpy clots all over it.

But Calvin knows that's *still* not quite the right word for his brother.
Close . . . but not yet.

Something is missing.

At bedtime, Calvin slides me under his bed.

I'm exhausted.

My spine is bent, my pages are dog-eared, my cover is limp. I need a break.
Even the page that **slumber** is on is wrinkled.

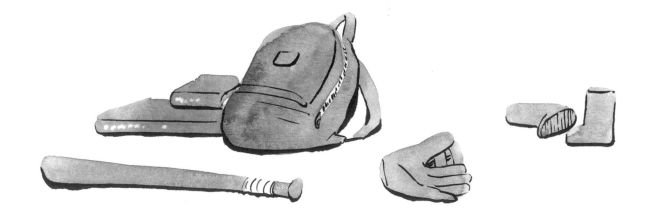

But then Calvin drags me out from under his bed, gets his glass of water, and tiptoes into his brother's room in the dark. Suddenly I'm not tired anymore.

Has Calvin *finally* figured out the right word to use for his brother?

I'm sure I already know which page to turn to, and I'm happy to riffle my pages to find it.

It's going to be soggy with water, but I don't care!

Prank!

That is the right word for his brother!

Hold on a second!

Calvin is laughing.

His brother is laughing, too. They high-five each other.

So now I'm looking for **hilarity** in my pages instead, when Calvin grabs me.

Quickly, he flips to a new page.

I'm wide awake now!

And there it is—the very best word:

FAMILY!

With love and aloha for the Adorables, who always know a good word when they see it:
Carson, Maren, Samantha, and Taylor. —M.S.

For everyone with a love of words. —M.D.

Text © 2020 by Margo Sorenson • Illustrations © 2020 by Mike Deas • Hardcover ISBN 978-0-88448-822-4

Tilbury House Publishers • www.tilburyhouse.com

Library of Congress Control Number: 2020939563 • Designed by Frame25 Productions • Printed in Korea • 15 16 17 18 19 20 XXX 10 9 8 7 6 5 4 3 2 1

Margo Sorenson is the author of more than thirty books for children from toddler age through high school. She enjoys author school visits, Zooms, and Skypes with classrooms. A mother, grandmother, and national award–winning former teacher, she has lived in Spain, Italy, Minnesota, Hawaii, and now California. You can visit Margo at www.margosorenson.com.

Mike Deas gets his flair for illustrative storytelling from an early love of reading and drawing. He fine-tuned his drawing skills and imagination at Capilano College's Commercial Animation Program in Vancouver, then worked as a concept artist, texture artist, and art lead in the video game industry in England and California before returning to his native British Columbia. Mike has illustrated several children's books including *The Buddy Bench* (Tilbury House, 2019) and *Gloria's Big Problem* (Tilbury House, 2020).

bewilderment (bi-'wil-dər-mənt) (n.) Complete confusion like the feeling I get in social studies class.

courageous (kə-'rā-jəs) (adj) Standing up to a bully even if you're afraid makes you courageous. Like me. HEY, what can I say?

hilarity (hi-'ler-a-tē) (n.) When your brother falls on his face (see prank) and it makes you laugh so hard you snort milk out your nose, that's hilarity!

mayhem ('mā-hem) (n.) A good word for the chaos on my school bus every morning. If you ride my bus, wear a hazmat suit!

prank (prank) (n.) When you tie your brother's shoelaces together under the table and then he tries to walk and falls flat on his face, that's a prank. Not that I'd do anything like that.